A Winning Goal

by Laurie Calkhoven

illustrated by Arcana Studios

American Girl®

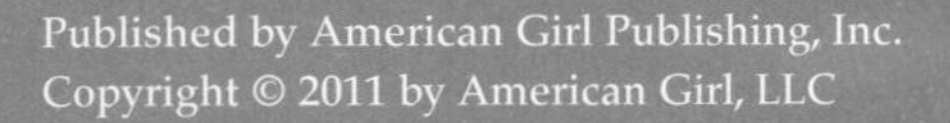

Published by American Girl Publishing, Inc.

Questions or comments? Call 1-800-845-0005, visit our Web site at americangirl.com, or write to Customer Service, American Girl, 8400 Fairway Place, Middleton, WI 53562-0497.

Printed in China
11 12 13 14 15 16 LEO 10 9 8 7 6 5 4 3 2

Illustrated by Thu Thai at Arcana Studios

Cataloging-in-Publication Data available from the Library of Congress

Welcome to Innerstar University! At this imaginary, one-of-a-kind school, you can live with your friends in a dorm called Brightstar House and find lots of fun ways to let your true talents shine. Your friends at Innerstar U will help you find your way through some challenging situations, too.

When you reach a page in this book that asks you to make a decision, choose carefully. The decisions you make will lead to more than 20 different endings! (*Hint:* Use a pencil to check off your choices. That way, you'll never read the same story twice.)

Want to try another ending? Read the book again—and then again. Find out what would have happened if you'd made *different* choices. Then head to www.innerstarU.com for even more book endings, games, and fun with friends.

Innerstar Guides

Every girl needs a few good friends to help her find her way. These are the friends who are always there for **you.**

Amber

An animal lover and a loyal friend

Neely

A creative girl who loves dance, music, and art

Logan

A super-smart girl who is curious about EVERYTHING

Shelby

A kind girl who is there for her friends—and loves making NEW friends!

Innerstar U Campus

1. Rising Star Stables
2. Star Student Center
3. Brightstar House
4. Starlight Library
5. Sparkle Studios
6. Blue Sky Nature Center

7. Real Spirit Center
8. Five-Points Plaza
9. Starfire Lake & Boathouse
10. U-Shine Hall
11. Good Sports Center
12. Shopping Square
13. The Market
14. Morningstar Meadow

You're dribbling the soccer ball down the field with minutes to go. The score is tied. You can hear fans cheering in the stands and your Innerstar U coach and teammates shouting encouragement: "Go, go, go!"

Members of the other team are shouting, too—urging each other to steal the ball from you. But you stay focused on the ball and the goal. That focus is what makes you one of the best players on your team.

The other team's defenders are closing in on you. You need to pass the ball or shoot for the goal. Riley, Innerstar U's team captain, is in position to accept a pass and take a shot at the goal.

Should you pass the ball to Riley? Or should you kick the ball and try to make the winning goal? You have a split second to make a decision.

If you take the shot yourself, turn to page 10.

If you pass the ball to Riley, turn to page 12.

You eye the goalkeeper and shift from foot to foot. You want to keep her guessing about what you're going to do. Then you reach back to give the ball a solid kick.

Suddenly you realize that from this angle, you're much more likely to send the ball out of bounds than into the net. You hesitate and lose your focus, just for a second. In that moment, a defender from the other team steals the ball.

"Good try!" Riley yells. She races down the field after the ball, ready to fight for it until the final whistle. You should race after her, but you feel as if you've already lost the game for your team. Then Riley intercepts a pass and starts dribbling toward you and the goal. You still have a chance!

"Go, Riley!" you yell.

Riley passes the ball to you, and your instincts kick in. You don't hesitate. You pivot and send the ball sailing right past the goalkeeper and into the net.

Score!

 Turn to page 13.

13
GO TEAM!

You pass the ball to Riley just as a defender on the other team tries to steal the ball. Your feet get tangled and the two of you end up facedown in the grass, but Riley is in the perfect position to collect your pass.

You look up in time to see Riley trap the ball. She's got defenders on her heels, but she's an expert at keeping the ball away from the other team.

"Go, Riley!" you yell.

The player from the other team groans—not because she's hurt, but because she suspects what's coming.

Paige and Neely are running on either side of Riley, blocking when they need to. Riley dribbles for a few feet and then takes the shot. Innerstar U scores just before the final whistle blows. You've won the game!

You help your opponent to her feet and then run down the field to celebrate with your teammates.

Turn to page 14.

"Woo-hoo!" you shout. You run down the soccer field cheering with the rest of your teammates. Winning is the best! It feels even better when *you're* the one who scored the winning goal.

Your friend Logan gives you a high five. "Way to go!" she says.

Paige is grinning from ear to ear. Neely and Isabel pull you into a group hug.

You're soaking up your coach's congratulations, too, when you spot Riley exchanging high fives with Emmy, another friend and teammate. Without Riley's super-quick thinking and expert passing, there's no way Innerstar U would have won the ball back in time for you to score a goal. Riley could have taken the shot herself, but instead she let you be the star.

You make a note to remember that the next time you have the choice to pass or shoot. Riley put the team first. When you had the same chance, you put yourself first, and the other team stole the ball.

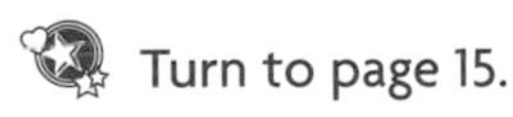
Turn to page 15.

Everyone crowds around Riley to congratulate her on the winning goal.

"Great shot, Riley," says your coach.

"That was super exciting," Neely says. "But next time, can we score more than half a second before the whistle blows? That was way too much drama!" Neely pretends to swoon into Isabel's arms.

"I'll see what I can do," Riley says with a laugh. Then she pulls you into the center of the circle. "Great work driving that ball down the field!" she says. "We couldn't have won the game without you."

You try to be modest, but you feel a big grin spreading across your face. You love being one of the best soccer players at Innerstar U. The only thing better than helping your friend make the winning goal would have been drilling the ball into the net yourself.

Still, it was nice that Riley shared the glory. *She could have hogged all the attention for herself*, you think. You're impressed and grateful that Riley called out your winning play, too.

Turn to page 16.

"Hooray for Riley—expert ball stealer!" you yell.

Riley takes a little bow, and then reaches out and steals the ball out of Emmy's hands. Emmy played goalkeeper today and made more than one great save.

Emmy grabs the ball back with a fake growl. Everyone cracks up.

"Hooray for *Emmy*!" Riley says. "Hooray for everybody! Great game."

That's the thing about Riley. She wants all the girls on the team to feel good about playing, whether they're the strongest players or not. Riley is a big part of why soccer is one of your favorite things to do at Innerstar U. You get to hang out and practice with your friends, wear a cool uniform, and win games.

You especially love winning games. And you have to admit that you love being one of the best players on the team. It feels great to know that you can come through for your teammates when it really counts—in the final moments of a game, just before that whistle blows.

Turn to page 16.

You, Paige, and Logan are the last ones out of the locker room. You walk together across campus toward the student center, where all of your teammates plan to meet up for a victory party.

As you walk with your friends, the conversation shifts to the attic at Brightstar House. It used to be filled with dusty old furniture, but now it's been cleared out. You're on the committee that will decide what to do with the attic, and there seem to be as many ideas for the space as there are girls at Innerstar U.

"I'd love to use it for study groups," Logan says.

"Or maybe a mini greenhouse," Paige suggests.

You smile. Paige's room is overflowing with plants. She has a major green thumb.

As you pass through Five-Points Plaza, you notice Riley standing by the fountain. She's peering over Shelby's shoulder, looking at the screen on Shelby's camera. Shelby brings her camera to every game.

Maybe she got a shot of the winning goal, you think. Paige and Logan run ahead to the party, but you stop to check out Shelby's photos.

Before you can even say hello, Riley says, "Great news! Shelby is joining the team."

Shelby gives you a big smile. "You guys look like you're having so much fun out there," she says. "I thought I'd give it a try."

"She hasn't played before," Riley adds. "Can you work with her—teach her what you know?"

Shelby's looking at you with a hopeful smile. You can tell she expects you to say yes, but you think for a minute before answering. Shelby's a good friend, but you're not so sure about your own coaching abilities. Plus, you're not sure that now—in the middle of a winning streak—is the right time to add a totally inexperienced player to the team.

 If you agree to coach Shelby, turn to page 20.

 If you reluctantly say no, turn to page 18.

Shelby was one of your first friends at Innerstar U. She invited you to a sleepover in your very first week, and the minute she heard you liked to play soccer, she introduced you to Riley. You've been on the team ever since.

You really hate to say no to Shelby and Riley. But even if this were a good time to add a new player to the team, you're not the right person to help Shelby. Between sports, homework, and the new attic project, you already have too much going on. Plus, you've never coached anyone before. You wish Riley hadn't asked you in front of Shelby. That puts you in an awkward spot.

"I'm sorry," you tell them. "I'm really busy right now. I'm probably not the best girl for the job."

Shelby's face falls, and Riley looks disappointed. You feel a twinge of guilt, but you're pretty sure you made the right decision. You change the subject by asking Shelby if you can see a few of her photos. Then you hurry on ahead to the victory party.

At team practice a couple of days later, Shelby struggles with basic skills like dribbling and passing. More than once, she touches the ball with her hands. If she makes mistakes like that in a game, they will lead to lots of free kicks—and maybe goals—for the other team.

Shelby is trying her best, but she has a lot to learn. Your coach pulls her aside to work with her while the rest of the team plays a practice game. Once again you wonder if *now* is the right time to add a new player to the team, especially with another tough game coming up.

The next afternoon, you're finishing up a workout at the Good Sports Center when you see Shelby and Amber, another fairly new player, kicking the ball around. You remember a couple of drills that helped you improve your skills when you first started playing. Should you run over to see if you can help?

 If you remind yourself that you're too busy, turn to page 22.

 If you stop to show Shelby and Amber one of the drills, turn to page 24.

You're worried about adding a new player to the team in the middle of the season, but you push those thoughts aside to help your friend. Shelby was the first person to welcome you to Innerstar U. She invited you to a sleepover and made you feel right at home.

"Welcome to the team!" you say. "I'd love to work with you, Shelby."

"Great! Where do we start?" Shelby asks.

"Equipment," you tell her. "We can't practice without shin guards. In soccer, you get kicked *a lot*."

Right after the party, you and Shelby head over to the Girl Gear shop and pick out a uniform in Shelby's size. You help her find shin guards and soccer cleats, too. By the time you leave the shop, Shelby is beaming. She's so excited about playing that you find yourself getting excited about being her coach. You're glad now that you said yes.

On your way back to Brightstar House, you set up some practice times. You say good-bye to Shelby at her door, and then you climb the stairs to the attic. You've been wanting to check out the space before your first committee meeting.

You were in the attic once before for a scavenger hunt, but it was so crowded with old furniture that you couldn't get a good look at it. It's empty now, except for a few crates and boxes, and it looks *huge*. Windows line both sides of the room. You could probably see the entire campus from those windows—once the dust and dirt are washed off.

This room has lots *of possibilities*, you think to yourself.

You're about to head back downstairs when Becca, one of your teammates, steps into the attic. Becca is a good soccer player, but she can be a sore loser. Luckily, after your team's win today, Becca seems to be in a great mood.

"Hey!" she says, skipping toward you across the empty attic. "I'm glad I ran into you. I've been thinking that this would make a perfect exercise room. Wouldn't it be great if we didn't have to head all the way across campus every time we wanted to work out?"

You nod. "Yeah, it sure would," you say.

"So will you support my idea in the attic committee meeting?" Becca asks, looking directly at you.

You cringe. You know that you should wait to hear everyone's ideas before agreeing to one, but you also know that Becca will grumble if you say no.

If you say yes to Becca, turn to page 25.

If you tell Becca you want to keep an open mind, turn to page 27.

You wave at Shelby and Amber, but you don't stop to play ball with them. You have way too much to do today.

All week long in soccer practice, you watch Shelby struggle. At the beginning of the next game, the coach puts Shelby in midfield. Today's game is against one of your toughest competitors. Every girl will have to play her best if you're going to win.

You overhear Becca, one of your teammates, talking to Riley. "Shelby's not ready to play in a game," Becca says. "She can't dribble or pass. She'll make us lose."

Riley shrugs. "Shelby needs the experience on the field," she says. "And it's not all about winning. It's about having fun."

Becca shakes her head. "It's not fair to the team if we lose because of one bad player," she says.

"It's not fair to the rest of the girls if we let only the best players into the game," Riley insists. "You get to be a good player by *playing*. That's good for the team—win or lose."

Becca doesn't say another word. As she turns and walks away, you can tell by the look on her face that she's frustrated. You don't blame her—you're worried, too. Shelby is clearly not ready to hit the field. She could make some big mistakes and end up feeling totally discouraged.

Turn to page 28.

U
7
U
3

You run over to Shelby and Amber and try to capture the ball. To your surprise, Shelby puts up a good fight. "Wow," you say. "You're starting to get the hang of this."

"It's really fun!" says Shelby.

"She's getting good, too," Amber says.

"How good are you two at *stealing* the ball?" you ask with a sly grin. You dribble toward the goal, trying to keep the ball away from Shelby and Amber. Amber manages to steal it from you, and then Shelby steals it from her.

Soon all three of you are giggling as you try to steal the ball from one another. By the time you start working on passing the ball, Emmy and Isabel have joined in, too. When Paige shows up, you have enough players for a three-on-three game. You, Shelby, and Amber lose, but you have a blast, and you learned a new move or two yourself!

 Turn to page 26.

"Turning this place into an exercise room is a good idea," you say.

"Great," Becca says. "Let's see if there are any other committee members who will support us. You're good friends with Emmy, right?"

You *are* good friends with Emmy, the project leader, but you're suddenly uncomfortable with the way Becca's going about things. She wants to get the whole group on her side before the first meeting. That doesn't seem right. You need to listen to everyone's ideas.

Still, you've got other things to think about right now, so you agree to mention Becca's plan to Emmy when you see her next. Then you start thinking about the soccer drills you'll run with Shelby tomorrow.

Turn to page 30.

You're tired but happy as you walk back to Brightstar House with Shelby. When she invites you to her room to watch a DVD about the U.S. women's soccer team, you say yes. Then an idea hits you. "Hey, what if we turned the attic into a TV room where we could hang out and watch DVDs?" you ask.

"Great idea!" says Shelby. "Let's bring it up at the meeting."

Shelby is being a good sport, especially considering the fact that you told her you were too busy to coach her. You feel the sudden urge to apologize.

"Hey, Shelby?" you say, reaching out for her arm so that she'll stop walking. "I'm sorry I said I couldn't coach you. You're a good friend. I should have made the time."

"No worries," Shelby says kindly. "I know you're busy."

"Not too busy to help out a teammate," you insist. "Passing drills? Same time tomorrow?"

"Okay," Shelby says. "But are you sure?"

"I'm sure," you say. You know Shelby would do the same for you.

Everyone has things to learn, you realize now. Shelby might need soccer training, but she's taught you—the star player—a lot about being a teammate *and* a good friend.

The End

"There are lots of ways we could use this space," you say to Becca. "Neely wants—"

Becca cuts you off. "But a gym is the best thing for the team," she says shortly.

"Maybe," you say. "But let's wait and hear what some of the other girls have to say before we decide on one idea."

Becca frowns. She's obviously angry with you, but you're not going to let her talk you into something you're not sure about.

"Right now, I'm seriously starving," you say, trying to lighten the mood. "Let's go have dinner."

Becca shakes her head. "I have a couple of things to do first," she says.

You wonder if that means talking to other committee members, but you can't worry about that now. You *are* hungry. On your way over to the Star Student Center, you run over some basic soccer drills in your mind. Tomorrow you'll start working with Shelby, and you want to be ready.

Turn to page 30.

Riley wins the coin toss for Innerstar U, and Emmy kicks the ball to start the game. The two of them drive the ball through midfield with quick passes. You hang back, ready to defend your goal if the other team intercepts.

When Riley reaches the other team's goal, she passes the ball to Emmy, who gives the ball a powerful kick. It bounces out of bounds. Now the other team starts dribbling the ball down the field.

"Block it, Shelby!" Paige yells.

Shelby tries, but she misses and falls over backward. You're so busy watching her that you take your eyes off the ball. Before you know it, the other team is past you, too.

They shoot. *Wham!* The ball sails past Amber, today's goalkeeper, and into your net. Score one for the other team.

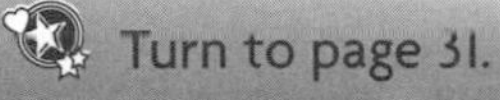

Turn to page 31.

When you arrive at the Good Sports Center for your first practice, Shelby is already suited up and kicking the ball around. As soon as your shin guards are in place, you start teaching Shelby some basic dribbling skills. You explain to her how important it is to be able to dribble with the insides and outsides of both feet.

Unfortunately, Shelby can't seem to dribble with either side of either foot. By the end of the hour, she's tired and frustrated—and so are you.

"Am I ever going to get this?" Shelby asks.

You pause. You don't want to discourage your friend this early on. You think back to when you first started to play soccer, and you remember that *you* weren't such a great dribbler either. "It takes time," you reassure Shelby. "I was clumsy when I first started. How about if tomorrow we work on passing? You might be really good at that."

Turn to page 32.

You should have blocked that pass. Becca shakes her head with disgust, and you cringe, waiting for her or the coach to let you have it. Riley claps her hands and shouts, "We'll get the next one!"

Thirty minutes later, the other team is leading 3 to 0. Shelby has been making all kinds of mistakes, and so have you. The more mistakes Shelby makes, the more tense you get. You're starting to feel as if neither one of you can do anything right.

At halftime, Riley pulls you aside. "Is something on your mind?" she asks. "You seem to be having trouble concentrating."

Riley's right. You can't focus. Your poor playing embarrasses you, but you think Shelby is the problem. You're so worried about her messing up—and about Becca's reaction—that you're messing up, too.

If you tell Riley how you feel, turn to page 33.

If you decide to focus on your own game, turn to page 36.

The next day after classes, you and Shelby take a lap around the soccer field to warm up. Then you get to work on a few passing drills.

Yesterday, you thought Shelby had trouble with dribbling. It turns out she's a better dribbler than she is a passer.

Shelby's working incredibly hard, but you're really beginning to wonder whether soccer is the right sport for her. Then you remind yourself that you've been playing for years and Shelby is just getting started. Are you expecting too much too soon?

You can see that Shelby is getting frustrated again. Her passes don't go where they're supposed to, but she does have a good, strong kick.

"Your kick is great," you say encouraginly. "I'll bet shooting goals will be your specialty."

Turn to page 34.

"I can't focus because I'm worried about Shelby's mistakes," you say to Riley. "Becca made a good point earlier. Are you and the coach sure it's a good idea to put a new player on the field during such an important game?"

Riley looks confused. "The game isn't as important as each of us doing our best and having a good time," she says. "Shelby needs time and experience on the field."

You don't know how to respond to Riley. You head back into the game, but you still can't seem to focus. You miss an easy pass and take a tumble. The other team scores—again.

You see Becca grumbling to one of her friends. Their eyes are on you.

Your coach runs over to see if you're all right. You're fine, but you could use this fall as an excuse to get out of the rest of the game. At least that will make Becca happy, and you won't feel as if the team's loss is your fault.

If you tell your coach you need to sit out the rest of the game, turn to page 39.

If you stay in the game, turn to page 36.

When you try to teach Shelby how to shoot the ball into the net, she has trouble with that, too. The ball goes over the top and to the side of the goal, but never *into* the goal. And when Shelby tries out the goalkeeper position, she ducks instead of keeping the ball out of the net.

After practice, Shelby blinks away tears of frustration.

"We'll keep trying," you comfort her. But you fear that she won't get the hang of soccer, and you wonder if it's fair to the team—or to Shelby—to put such a new player on the field. You decide to talk to Riley about it.

Turn to page 37.

You try to stop worrying about Shelby and Becca and to focus instead on doing your own job on the field. After a few more plays, Shelby starts to get the rhythm of the game. When she intercepts a pass, you're the first one to run over to give her a high five. Even Becca seems impressed. Maybe your team can pull it together and win this game after all!

By the final few minutes of the game, Innerstar U is trailing by just one goal. The other team's offense has the ball and is bearing down on you. If they make this goal, Innerstar U has no chance of winning.

A pass comes in your direction. You almost trip over your own feet trying to steal the ball, but you manage to gain control of it. Now you need to pass the ball. Shelby is in the best position in the midfield, but you can see your teammate Paige, too, and she's a stronger player.

If you pass the ball to Paige, turn to page 38.

If you pass the ball to Shelby, turn to page 41.

When you get back to Brightstar House, you tell Shelby you'll see her later at the attic meeting. Then you knock on Riley's door. She opens it quickly, as if she was already on her way out. She's carrying a clipboard under her arm.

"I was just about to look for you!" Riley says. "Coach and I need to make up the team list for Saturday's game. Is Shelby better at offense or defense?"

You hesitate. You honestly can't think of any position that Shelby would be comfortable in.

Riley can tell that you're struggling with your answer. "Is something wrong?" she asks.

"Shelby's working really hard," you say. "But I don't know if she's ready to play in a real game."

Riley pauses, tapping her pen on her clipboard. "Maybe she needs to play a practice game first," she says. "I'll bet you could use the field Friday afternoon."

"That's a good idea," you say.

"Or maybe," Riley goes on, "we should just ask Shelby how she feels. If she doesn't feel ready, she could sit out the first game."

You nod slowly. That's a good idea, too. You don't want to hurt Shelby's feelings, though, by making her think that *you* don't think she's ready to play.

 If you decide to start pulling together a practice game after the attic meeting ends, turn to page 42.

 If you decide to talk with Shelby first, turn to page 40.

Your opponents are crowding Paige, but you know she's better at driving the ball down the field than Shelby is. You kick the ball in Paige's direction. One of the midfielders guarding her intercepts your pass. Before you know it, the other team scores. Innerstar U has lost the game.

"I'm sorry," you tell Riley as you jog off the field. "I guess I should have passed the ball to Shelby."

Riley is upbeat, as always. "We all make mistakes," she says. "We'll get 'em next time. You did a great job getting your focus back in the second half."

You're totally relieved. Riley could have blamed you for losing the game. Instead, she made a point of telling you what you did right. You feel better already.

Riley's attitude makes you realize how important it is to tell Shelby what *she* did right, too. At the postgame party, you'll try to make Shelby feel just as good as Riley made you feel. Isn't that what friends—and teammates—are for?

The End

"I hurt my ankle," you tell the coach. "I'd better sit out the rest of the game."

The truth is, your ankle does hurt a little bit. You know the pain will probably be gone soon, but you can't focus. Becca's muttered insults are distracting—especially when they're about you. You watch the rest of the game from the sidelines, cringing every time Shelby makes a mistake. When your team loses, you're not at all surprised.

You come up with excuses to sit out the next two games, too. You really miss playing, but you don't want to feel like a loser, either. Sitting on the bench, you can tell yourself that the team's losses are not your own.

You're sitting on the sidelines watching a game when it occurs to you that Shelby is getting much better. You know she has been determined to improve her playing, and some of the other girls on the team have been practicing with her. You can see that Shelby's hard work is paying off. In the last few seconds of the game, she passes the ball to Paige. Paige turns and slams the ball right into the goal.

Turn to page 44.

Riley goes with you to talk to Shelby, which is a big relief. Riley is always celebrating other girls' strengths and accomplishments. You know she'll make Shelby feel good.

You catch Shelby in her room, getting ready to head to the attic for the meeting.

"Hey, teammates," she says with a smile. "What's going on?"

Riley speaks right up, thank goodness. "I've heard how hard you've been practicing," she says to Shelby. "How do you feel about playing in Saturday's game? Do you think you're ready?"

Shelby's smile fades. She bites her lip and glances at you, and then back at Riley.

Turn to page 53.

Your pass goes wide. Shelby races for it, but the other team manages to gain control. They're halfway down the field when the final whistle blows.

As you and your teammates leave the field, Riley pats Shelby on the back. "Good game," she says.

Shelby doesn't respond. You glance up and see that her eyes are filled with tears. "I'm sorry," Shelby says quietly. "It's my fault we lost."

"No one played a perfect game," Riley says, putting her arm around Shelby. "Don't blame yourself."

Shelby nods, but she packs up and leaves in a rush. You can tell she still thinks the loss is her fault. *Is that because I made her feel as if I didn't want her on the team?* you wonder. You've been unfair to Shelby, and it's time to apologize.

You find Shelby in her room, looking at a stack of soccer photos with a troubled expression. You sit down next to her and take a deep breath. "I sent you a terrible pass," you say sincerely. "No one could have trapped that ball."

"Really?" Shelby asks, looking up from the photos.

You nod. "In fact, I could use some extra practice on my passing," you say. "Want to kick the ball around later?"

A slow smile spreads across your friend's face. "That would be fun," she says.

Fun. Making friends and having fun are the reasons you joined the soccer team in the first place. It took Shelby to remind you of that, and you're sure glad she did.

The End

You feel much better after your talk with Riley. You hurry back to your room so that you can change your clothes before the attic meeting begins.

When you climb the stairs to the attic, you find a roomful of girls waiting for the meeting to start. Becca waves you over. "You're going to speak up for my gym idea, right?" she asks eagerly.

You know this idea is important to Becca. You even mentioned it to Emmy over breakfast this morning. Still, you're starting to feel as if Becca is bullying you into making a decision. Luckily, Emmy calls the meeting to order before you have to say so to Becca.

When Emmy invites everyone to share ideas for how to use the attic, Logan raises her hand. Emmy calls on her, but Becca jumps in first.

"This place would make a great gym," Becca says. "Those of us who want to work out don't always have time to run over to the sports center. If this were a gym, we could just run upstairs." Becca looks at you, waiting for you to agree.

"That's a good idea," you say. "But I want to hear the other ideas, too."

Every time someone throws out an idea, Becca interrupts to say why hers is better. Before you know it, everyone is talking at once, and you can't make out what anybody is saying above the noise.

Turn to page 45.

You cheer when the team wins, but you also feel a little sad—not to mention embarrassed. You secretly agreed with Becca when she said Shelby wasn't ready to play, but you know now that Riley was right. Shelby just needed a little practice and teammates who believed in her. *You* were the one who let the team down with your fake excuses. You made winning more important than having fun and being a good teammate.

At the victory celebration, you find Riley and apologize for missing the last couple of games. She's sweet about it, of course, and says she hopes you'll be on the field for the next one.

"I hope I'm not too rusty after a couple of weeks of not playing," you say.

Shelby, who just walked over for another slice of pizza, overhears you. "Amber and I are going to practice tomorrow afternoon," she says. "Want to join us?"

"Wow, that would be great," you say. You're relieved that Riley and Shelby are willing to give you a second chance. This time, you're determined not to let them down.

The End

By the end of the meeting, it feels as if you've gotten nowhere. Emmy holds up her hand to try to call everyone back to attention.

"I think it's great that so many of you have ideas," Emmy says with a laugh, "but it's almost time for dinner, and we're never going to figure this out today." She runs a finger through the dust on a windowsill. "One thing I think we can all agree on, though, is that we need to do some major cleaning up here."

"That's for sure," Logan says. Everyone else is nodding, too, except Becca. She crosses her arms and says nothing.

"Once we've got the attic cleaned up, we can talk more about the best way to use the space," Emmy says. "Let's get started Friday night. If we work hard, we might be able to finish up after the soccer game on Saturday."

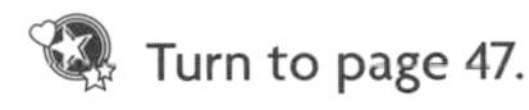
Turn to page 47.

When Shelby arrives for practice the next day, she finds you and Amber in the middle of the field. You've set up orange cones for her to weave through as she dribbles.

"What's this?" Shelby asks excitedly.

You answer her by tossing her a ball. "Follow me," you say with a grin. You dribble your own ball through the cones, and Shelby jumps in quickly behind you.

Once Shelby gets the hang of cutting in and out of the cones, you invite her to play Monkey in the Middle. You, Amber, and Shelby take turns being the monkey, who has to try to intercept a pass between the other two players. After that, you move over to the gymnastic mats so that Shelby can practice diving for the ball and jumping to block goals without getting hurt.

The three of you have a great time practicing your moves. You know Shelby is having a blast, but she's also learning a lot, too. You can't wait to see how she does in the practice game!

Turn to page 52.

After dinner, you set out to recruit some of your friends for a practice game of soccer. You've decided to ask your soccer-playing friends for some coaching ideas, too. You and Shelby can use all the help you can get.

You walk toward the library, where some of your friends like to study. On the way there, you spot a poster for a dance recital. Your friend Neely is going to dance a solo. She's one of the most talented and creative people you know. Maybe she'll have some coaching ideas for you.

Then you hear a dog bark from across campus. It's been a while since you stopped by Pet-Palooza. Should you take a break from soccer and go visit the animals?

If you continue on to the library, turn to page 48.

If you go looking for Neely, turn to page 50.

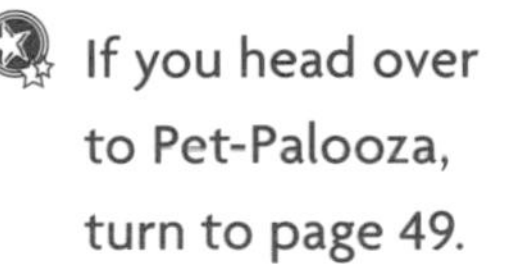
If you head over to Pet-Palooza, turn to page 49.

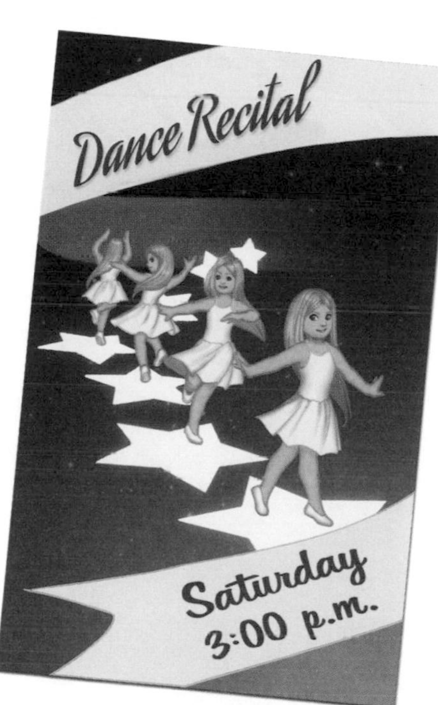

At Starlight Library, you find your friend Logan curled up in a window seat, reading a book about Antarctica. She always seems to be learning something new.

You invite Logan to take part in your practice game, and then you confide in her. "I don't know if Shelby will *ever* learn how to play soccer," you admit.

Logan thinks for a moment. "Different people learn in different ways," she says. "Shelby's a photographer. Maybe we can find some soccer photos and DVDs for her to study!"

With Logan's help, you find lots of things for Shelby. You drop them off at her room and then tell her about the practice game you're putting together. Shelby seems pretty excited—and relieved—to hear that she'll have the chance to practice her skills before a real game.

Turn to page 52.

Your friend Amber is a volunteer at Pet-Palooza, a pet day-care center on campus. She's always happy to have help training and grooming the animals, and she understands that sometimes a girl needs some love from a furry friend.

Today you find Amber exercising some of the pups. Pepper, a young husky, is running through an agility course—weaving through cones, jumping small hurdles, and running through a tunnel. He looks as if he's having a blast!

"It's great exercise for dogs," Amber explains. "They have fun and learn a lot at the same time. Pepper especially loves running the course. He's a ball of energy."

Suddenly, a lightbulb goes on in your head. "Wow," you say. "I've been drilling Shelby on soccer skills, but I haven't thought about ways to make the drills more fun for her. I'll try that. I bet it will make a big difference!"

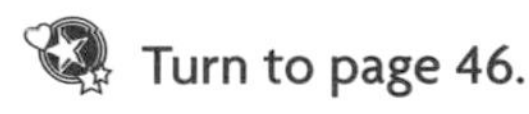
Turn to page 46.

You're not surprised to find Neely in one of the dance studios at U-Shine Hall. After you recruit her for your practice game, you ask her for coaching ideas.

"For me, everything's easier with music," Neely says. "Especially when I'm learning something new. Have you tried practicing to music? If you think about it, dribbling is kind of like dancing." She pretends to dribble an imaginary ball across the dance floor, which makes you giggle.

You decide to give Neely's idea a try during tomorrow's practice with Shelby. "Want to join us?" you ask Neely.

"Definitely. I'll bring my dancing shoes," she jokes.

The next afternoon, Neely meets you and Shelby at Morningstar Meadow with a CD player. You practice to music, stopping to dance when you need a break.

Shelby loves dancing, so the music perks her up—even after an hour of practice, when you know she must be tired. With Neely's help, soccer practice has become much more fun. You can tell that Shelby is improving!

 **Turn to page 52.**

4
8

On Friday afternoon, Logan, Paige, Neely, and Amber meet you and Shelby at the sports center for a three-on-three practice game. Shelby will get some great experience on the field today, and you'll be able to tell if she's ready for a real competition. That's a good thing, since tomorrow's game will be a tough one.

A few minutes into the practice game, you can tell that Shelby is playing a little better. Looking for fun new ways to teach her has paid off. Taking part in an "almost real" game seems to be boosting her confidence, too, but she's still making lots of mistakes.

The two of you are cooling off by Starfire Lake after the practice game when Riley joins you. She's carrying a duffel bag and a clipboard.

"Ready for tomorrow's big game?" Riley asks.

Instead of answering, Shelby looks to you for guidance. Your stomach twists. You don't want to shake her new-found confidence, but you're worried about tomorrow's game. Shelby has been working hard, and she has come a long way. But is she ready to play in a competition?

 If you admit that you don't think Shelby is quite ready, turn to page 54.

 If you suggest a position for Shelby, turn to page 55.

"I don't think I'm ready for a real game," Shelby finally says. She looks at you apologetically. "You've been so great about coaching me. I didn't want to hurt your feelings by telling you I didn't think I was up to playing."

Your jaw drops. "Really?" you say. "But I was feeling the same way! You've been working *so* hard. I didn't want to make you feel bad by telling you that Saturday's game might be too soon for you to play."

After hearing your words, Shelby looks as relieved as you feel. She starts giggling.

Riley laughs, too. "Looks like you both agree after all," she says.

Shelby nods. Then she gives you a serious look. "I *have* come a long way because of your coaching," she says. "But I want to feel strong and confident when I play my first game, and I'm not there yet."

"That makes sense," you say. "Let's just promise to be honest with each other from now on—and to keep practicing until you *are* ready."

"Agreed!" says Shelby. She reaches out and gives your hand a playful shake. Then you, Shelby, and Riley head to the committee meeting with your arms linked—true teammates.

The End

"What do you think, Coach?" Shelby asks with a smile. "Am I ready to play?"

Your eyes dart uneasily from Shelby to Riley and back again. You say nothing.

Shelby's face falls, and Riley cocks her head at you, clearly confused. "What's the problem?" she asks.

You can't look either one of them in the eye, so you stare at the water. "I'm not sure Shelby's ready," you say. "It's a big game. There'll be a lot of pressure on us to win."

"It's not all about winning," Riley replies shortly. Then she asks Shelby, "Are you having fun playing soccer?"

Shelby nods, but you can tell that you've taken some of the joy out of the game for her. "It's been fun," she says, "but I don't want to be the reason we lose."

"No *one* person can make a team lose," Riley says firmly. "Just like no one person can make a team win."

Turn to page 56.

You suggest a position where you think Shelby will feel the least amount of pressure. "I think Shelby will do best in midfield," you tell Riley.

"Great! I'll tell the coach," Riley says, making a note on her clipboard. "Maybe we can put both of you in midfield."

You prefer to play forward—forwards get to make the most goals—but you know it's only fair to try out all the positions and let your teammates do the same. Besides, if you're in midfield with Shelby, maybe you can catch some of her mistakes before they lead to goals for the other team.

Shelby smiles. "I'm glad you'll be playing next to me," she says. "I'll need the support!"

"You'll do fine," you tell her, trying to sound upbeat.

"It's going to be a great game," Riley says. "C'mon, let's go have dinner and fuel up for it."

As you walk toward the student center, you try to shake off your worry. After dinner, you'll be helping your friends clean the attic. If only your worries about the soccer game could be wiped away with soap and a little bit of elbow grease!

 Turn to page 57.

Now you feel awful. Shelby was excited to play in the game tomorrow, and you've ruined it for her. Riley seems pretty upset with you, too.

"C'mon," says Riley, pulling Shelby to her feet. "We can talk about it on the way to dinner." Riley glances at you to see if you're coming, too.

"You two go," you say. "I have to stop at the library." You don't really—you just need time to think.

You walk the path slowly, turning Riley's words over and over in your mind. *She's right*, you realize. You were so focused on winning that you forgot about having fun. You think back to when you first started playing soccer. You joined the team because you wanted to have fun. Shelby should have the same chance.

You catch up with Shelby as she's waiting in line for dinner. "Riley's right," you say to her. "The way you get to be a good player is by playing. You *have* to play in tomorrow's game."

Shelby hesitates, and then she gives you a nervous smile. "Okay," she says. "I'll try my best."

You feel a rush of relief. You'll try your best, too—to have fun on the field, and to help Shelby do the same.

The End

By the time you hit the attic after dinner, Emmy has brought up the cleaning supplies. Everybody pitches in—sweeping the floor, dusting the windowsills, and scrubbing the windows. You're amazed at how much you can do in just a short time when you all work together. You can't help noticing, though, that Becca is doing more whispering than cleaning. She's still trying to convince everyone that her idea is best.

It's just beginning to get dark when you finish. Logan peers out a window. "Look at the stars," she says. "We need to bring a telescope up here."

"A telescope?" Neely asks. "How about a CD player? This would make a great dance studio." She does a series of twirls across the now clean floor.

Emmy claps to get everyone's attention. "Great job!" she says. "Let's meet here tomorrow afternoon to paint, and then we can figure out how we'll use the space."

Tomorrow. You suddenly remember the soccer game. As you climb down the stairs from the attic, you start feeling sick to your stomach. How will Shelby do? Is she ready?

Turn to page 58.

Morning comes way too quickly. You get dressed and hurry to the sports center. Shelby is already there. She gives you a nervous smile.

As the announcer introduces the players, you and Shelby run onto the field. You feel yourself getting pumped up, listening to the cheering crowd.

"Wow!" Shelby says, taking in the fans in the bleachers.

"I know," you say. "Pretty cool, isn't it?"

After a team cheer, you and Shelby take your positions in midfield. The ref blows the whistle, and the game begins.

In the first few minutes, Emmy kicks the ball toward Shelby.

If you run over and collect the pass, turn to page 60.

If you let Shelby collect the pass, turn to page 61.

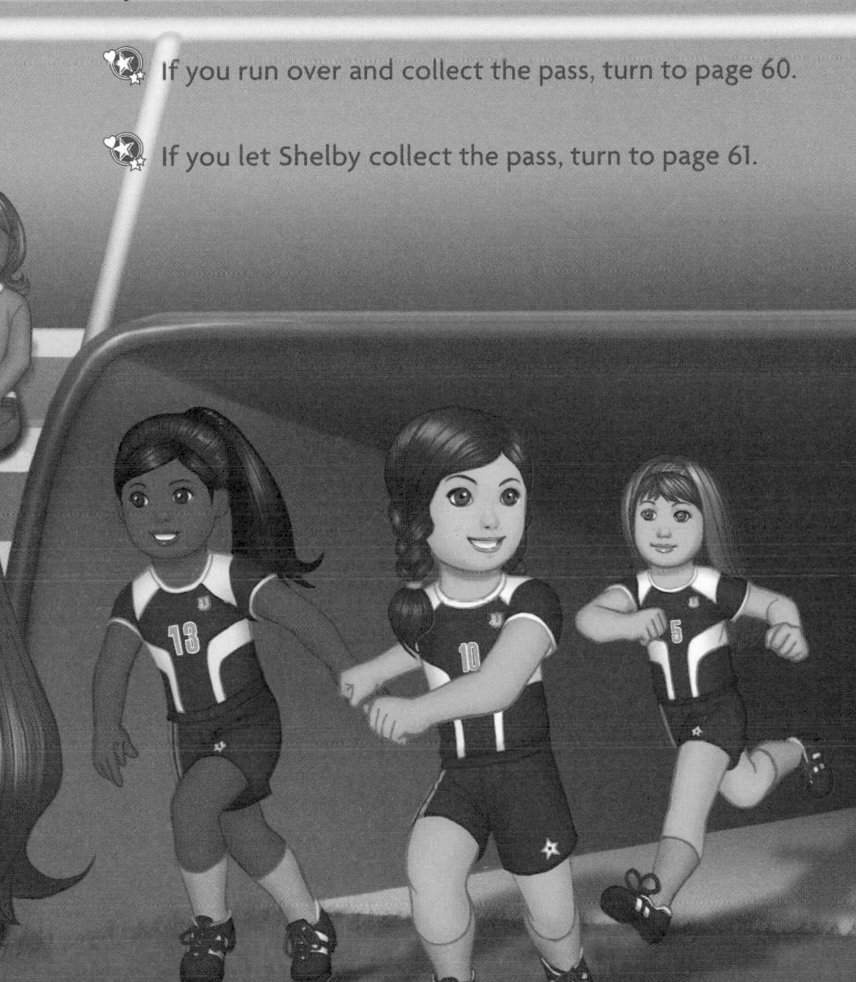

"Got it!" you yell, running over to take the pass. You dribble the ball for a few yards and then pass it to Paige, who is playing forward today.

You're at Shelby's side for the whole game. Every time the ball comes anywhere near her, you're ready to take it and dribble it down the field or pass it to another player.

Before you know it, the game's over. Innerstar U lost, but you're relieved that neither you nor Shelby had any major errors. Some days—like today—the other team just plays better.

As you jog off the field, you congratulate Shelby on making it through her first game. When she glances up at you, the look on her face nearly stops you in your tracks. She's clearly frustrated. "What's wrong?" you ask.

"My feet never touched the ball," Shelby says hotly. "Every time it came anywhere near me, you took control. I wanted to join the team so that I could *play* soccer. I might as well have been on the sidelines taking pictures."

Wow. You feel as if someone just dumped cold water on your head. But you know Shelby is right. You were so busy trying to make sure that she didn't make any mistakes that you didn't let her get near the ball.

Turn to page 62.

Instead of running to the ball, Shelby waits for it to come to her. The other team steals it easily.

"Good try!" you yell to Shelby. But the next time the ball heads toward her, you run to collect it. You and Shelby end up in a tangled pile of arms and legs while the other team intercepts the pass and scores.

Shelby makes one error after another. She just can't seem to relax enough to get into the rhythm of the game. She seems to have forgotten everything she learned. Twice she touches the ball with her hands.

After Innerstar U loses the game, Shelby forces a smile, but you can tell she's blinking back tears. "I should donate my uniform to someone who can actually *play* soccer," she says to you. "I think I should quit the team before I do any more damage."

You don't know what to say. Shelby did make some mistakes, but were they all her fault? You remember how patient Riley was with you when you first joined the team. You learned a lot from her then. Could Shelby's problem be that you're a bad coach?

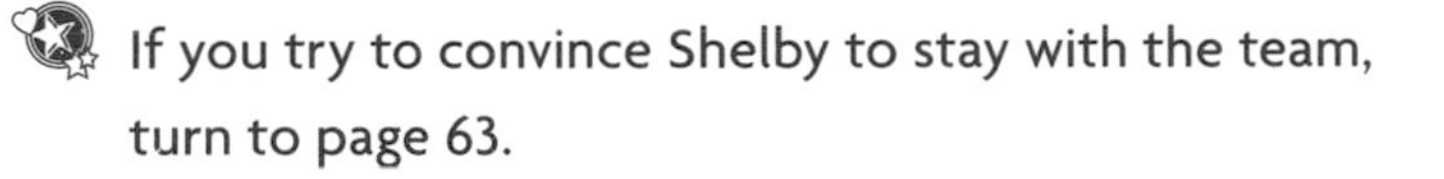
If you try to convince Shelby to stay with the team, turn to page 63.

If you tell Shelby she needs a better coach, turn to page 64.

If you let Shelby quit the team, turn to page 65.

Shelby must realize how bad you feel, because her tone softens. "I know you were trying to help me," she says. "But it's not fair to tell me I'm ready to play if you don't really think I am."

"You're right," you say quickly. "I'm sorry. I guess I was afraid of hurting your feelings. I thought if you made a lot of mistakes, you might give up."

"Mistakes?" says Riley, coming up from behind you. "We all make mistakes. We just have to learn from them."

Riley's right, too. You made plenty of mistakes when you first started to play, but those experiences made you a better player. Shelby needs to have the same chances. Next time, you'll give her an opportunity to really play—if she's willing to come back and try again.

"I hope you'll stick around for the next game," you say gently. "I'm really looking forward to playing *with* you instead of *for* you." You're relieved when Shelby smiles.

"I won't give up on myself that easily," Shelby says. "That is, if you won't."

"I won't," you promise her. "From now on, I'll be your coach, not your secret shadow. Deal?"

Shelby giggles as she says, "Deal."

The End

"Don't give up," you say. "You've worked so hard. I'd hate to see you quit after just one game."

"I made us lose," Shelby says flatly. She seems too frustrated to even talk about staying with the team.

"Will you wait a few days?" you ask. "Give yourself time to think about it."

Shelby shrugs. "I guess so," she says reluctantly.

As you and Shelby walk back across campus, Riley catches up with you. She's on her way to the Real Spirit Center to do some yoga, and she invites you and Shelby to join her. "It's a great way to stretch after a game," Riley explains.

You're surprised when Shelby agrees to yoga. Just ten minutes into class, you're also surprised by how flexible she is. You feel stiff as a board. By the time class ends, Shelby seems relaxed, and you're the one who's frustrated. Then it hits you—maybe Shelby should do yoga *before* soccer games. She'd feel less nervous, and she'd probably play better, too.

As you roll up your mat after class, you ask Riley if the whole team can do a little yoga before the next game. She thinks it's a great idea, and Shelby seems excited about it, too. As the three of you walk to Brightstar House, you can tell that Shelby is feeling better. You shoot Riley a grateful smile.

Turn to page 66.

"I'm not sure your playing is the problem," you tell Shelby. "It could be my coaching. Maybe Riley can find someone else to work with you—a better coach than me."

"No way!" Shelby says. "You've worked really hard. Don't give up on coaching just because your first try didn't work out."

You smile. "Those are great words of wisdom," you say, throwing your arm around her. "Don't give up on soccer just because your first *game* didn't work out."

Shelby shakes her head. "You're a much better coach than I am a player," she insists.

You squeeze Shelby's shoulders. "Please give yourself a second chance," you say. "At least give it one more game. Coach's orders."

Shelby hesitates, but you can see a smile starting to form at the corners of her mouth.

"I'll keep trying if you will," you promise.

Finally, Shelby nods. "Okay," she says, giving you a real smile now. "Want to kick the ball around later?" she asks.

"I can't wait," you tell her, and it's true. You feel great about helping Shelby get her confidence back, and you're feeling more confident now, too. Maybe Shelby's right—you're not such a bad coach after all.

The End

You don't try to talk Shelby out of quitting. You can see how frustrated she is. You go with her to tell Riley.

"This is my first and last soccer game," Shelby says to Riley. "I'll stick to taking pictures from the sidelines."

Riley seems confused. "But you looked like you were having fun out there," she says.

"I was, for a while," admits Shelby. "Then I made all those mistakes. I don't want to keep making the team lose."

Riley shakes her head. "No one player can win or lose a game," she says. "We're a team. *You're* a part of the team."

If you agree with Riley, turn to page 73.

If you remain silent, turn to page 69.

You and Shelby grab a bite to eat and then head upstairs for the attic-painting party. Emmy and Paige are already at work painting around the windows. You grab a paintbrush and head for the far wall.

When Becca sees you coming, she turns her back. She's probably disappointed that you didn't speak up for her idea. You're sorry she's upset, but you know that waiting to hear everyone's ideas was the right thing to do.

You try to apologize, but Becca won't listen. "Don't worry about it," she snaps. "Lots of other girls are on my side about the gym thing."

Becca stomps away, but it's hard to stay stressed about that for too long. Everyone else is working together and singing to the radio. Some of the girls start singing into their paintbrushes as if they're microphones, and you and Shelby join in. Soon your mood is as bright as the sun shining through the windows.

When you finish painting, the attic looks fabulous—with some walls painted bright blue and others a deep purple. Now it's time to figure out how to use the space. Emmy suggests that you spend the next week talking to the other girls on campus about what they would like to do with the attic. Then you can come together next weekend to share what you've learned.

Turn to page 70.

Shelby needs the practice on the field, so you kick the ball in her direction. You let out a big whoop when she traps the ball, but now Shelby has to decide whether to pass or dribble. She starts to drive the ball down the field.

"Go, Shelby!" you yell.

Your heart's in your throat as you run down the field beside Shelby. Then you see that Riley is open and just a few yards away. "Pass to Riley!" you yell.

Shelby does. Her pass goes wide, but Riley manages to get to the ball.

The play gives Shelby a shot of confidence. Suddenly, she's a more assertive player than she has been in practice. The next chance she gets, she intercepts a pass and sends it right to Riley. Then Riley kicks the ball straight into the net!

Not only did Innerstar U score, but Shelby got the assist! You're proud of and excited for your friend, and also a little bit proud of yourself. Shelby's turning into a great player, which means that *you* are turning into a pretty good coach, too.

The End

Shelby looks at you, her eyebrows raised in question. You can tell that she wants you to urge her to stay with the team, but you're not so sure that Riley is right. Shelby was really struggling on the field.

Riley is looking at you, too, but you stay silent.

Shelby blinks and looks away. "I know, I'm hopeless. I'd better quit now," she tells Riley before trudging away, totally discouraged.

Riley watches her walk away and then turns to you. Her mouth is set in an angry line. "Why didn't you say anything?" she asks.

You know you hurt Shelby's feelings, but you try to defend yourself. "She wasn't ready to play," you insist. "She made some big mistakes. It's part of why we lost."

"But since you're her coach, the first thing you need to teach her is that having fun is more important than winning," Riley says firmly. "*Friends* are more important than winning."

If you see Riley's point of view, turn to page 76.

If you wonder if you should quit the team too, turn to page 74.

All week, you and Shelby practice together. By the end of the week, with another game right around the corner, Shelby is playing much better and seems more confident.

The morning of game day, Shelby seems a little nervous, but Riley's yoga routine really helps. Not only are Shelby's muscles stretched and ready to play, but she's also a lot more relaxed than she was for her first game.

This time, you both take positions as defenders. Your midfielders do a great job of keeping the ball away from the goal, but then a shot breaks through. *How will Shelby do under pressure?* you wonder. You watch her slide to block a shot for a goal, and she misses.

Emmy, today's goalkeeper, makes the save and punches the ball right to you. You trap the ball, but members of the other team surround you. You need to pass, but to whom?

If you pass the ball to Shelby, turn to page 68.

If you pass the ball back to Emmy, turn to page 72.

10
5
3
4
8

You fake out the other team by moving your foot in front of the ball. They expect you to dribble or to pass the ball to Shelby, but instead, you pass the ball backward to Emmy. She can give the ball a powerful kick and send it down the field to Riley or Paige.

The only problem? Your kick fakes out Emmy, too. She isn't expecting a shot from her own teammate. Instead of blocking the ball, she freezes, and the ball goes right past her. You score a goal—for the other team!

By halftime, Innerstar U is down 3 to 0. At least one of those goals is your fault, but Shelby made lots of errors, too. *Am I a bad coach?* you wonder.

Riley does her best to rally the team, but by now, your confidence is pretty shaky. All the girls seem to be messing up, and you lose the game 4 to 0.

As you and your teammates congratulate the other team on their win, you overhear Riley invite them to the postgame party. You love to celebrate wins, but you're not in the mood for a party today.

"C'mon," Riley says. "It'll be fun."

If you skip the party and head to your room, turn to page 77.

If you go to the party, turn to page 75.

Riley's words make you realize that Shelby was too quick to give up on herself, and you were too quick to give up on her, too. "Riley's right," you tell Shelby. "*You* didn't lose the game. The team did. We all made mistakes."

Shelby hesitates. You can tell she's still torn between quitting and staying.

"C'mon," you say to Shelby with a smile. "I think we both need a second chance—you as a player and me as a coach. Please?" You give Shelby your best puppy-dog eyes.

Slowly, Shelby returns your smile. "Okay," she finally says. "For you."

"For me *and* you," you correct her. "We're a team, remember?" You're looking at Shelby, but you're really talking to yourself. Over the last couple of weeks, *you* forgot what it meant to be part of a team. You won't forget again.

The End

"Maybe I'm the one who should quit the team," you say. You wait for Riley to urge you to stay. She doesn't. Now you know how Shelby felt a moment ago—terrible. Your eyes fill with hot tears.

Riley's expression softens. "If you quit the team, it'll be our loss," she says gently. "But you'll lose even more. You love soccer."

You do love soccer. Sure, you're happier when you win than when you lose. But would you keep playing even if you lost every game? You don't even have to think about it now. You *would* keep playing. Being a member of a team and running around on the field are two things you love more than winning. Friends are another. You forgot that.

"I do love soccer," you admit. "But I love my friends more. I'm going to go find Shelby and apologize—and try to talk her into giving me another chance."

 Turn to page 78.

You don't feel like joining the party, but you want to be a good sport. On your way to the student center, you and Shelby lead the other team through Five-Points Plaza and show them the star-shaped fountain. Then you show them the beautiful lake and boathouse. Your mood starts to lift. You love showing off Innerstar U's cool campus.

Your mood brightens even more when a girl on the other team congratulates Shelby on one of her passes. "That blew right past me," the girl says.

You have no idea what pass she's talking about. *I was so worried about Shelby's mistakes that I missed the good things,* you think.

"I have an amazing coach," Shelby says, patting you on the back.

You feel a twinge of guilt. An amazing coach would have noticed Shelby's great pass.

You and Shelby both made some mistakes, but you did some things right, too. *From now on,* you tell yourself, *I'll try to focus on the things we do right.* You grab Shelby's hand and walk side by side with her to the party. It's time to celebrate a few great plays.

The End

Suddenly, you're ashamed of yourself. You've been focused on the wrong things, and you really hurt Shelby's feelings. You weren't a very good coach—or friend—to her.

"You're right," you tell Riley. "I'm sorry. I'm going to try to find Shelby and persuade her to stay on the team. Will you come with me?"

"Sure," Riley says. "We'll double-team her. She'll have to say yes."

Riley smiles, which puts you at ease. She doesn't seem angry anymore.

Together you set off in search of Shelby. As you walk across campus, you search your memory for ways to help Shelby have more fun on the field, too. *What made soccer fun for me when I was just starting out?* you ask yourself. You're determined to think of some ways to encourage your friend.

Turn to page 79.

Instead of celebrating, you trudge across campus to your room and plop down on a chair feeling like a loser. You keep thinking about the mistakes you made. Then you move on to Shelby's mistakes, and how you could have helped her play better.

You're still dwelling on the game when you hear voices in the hall. It's your team, coming back from the party. *Why do they sound so happy?* you wonder. *We lost!*

You overhear Riley encouraging Shelby. "We had fun, didn't we?" she says. "And you had a couple of really great plays out there. Nice job, Shelby."

Wow, you think. *Riley really doesn't mind losing. And she's doing her best to make sure that Shelby feels good about her game.* You realize that, as Shelby's coach, you should have been encouraging her, too.

Now you're embarrassed. You were so focused on your mistakes—and Shelby's—that you completely abandoned her after the game. And you forgot the basic rules of good sportsmanship. Shelby isn't the only one who needs some coaching. You do, too.

At the next practice, you decide, you're going to point out everything Shelby does *right* instead of trying to fix her mistakes. And after the next game—win or lose—you'll be out there, on the other side of this door, celebrating with your team.

The End

You find Shelby in the yearbook office at the student center. She's looking at soccer photos on a computer screen. You glance over her shoulder and take a peek at the photos.

"Those are great shots," you say.

Shelby glances up, sees you, and then turns back to the computer screen. "At least I'm good at *something*," she says.

"You're good at lots of things," you say quietly. "You'll be good at soccer, too, if you keep at it. I'm sorry I wasn't more encouraging. I really do want you to stay with the team."

"No," Shelby says quickly. "I'm finished with soccer."

If you accept Shelby's decision, turn to page 86.

If you urge her to stay with the team, turn to page 82.

You find Shelby at Five-Points Plaza. She's sitting on the edge of the fountain—the same place you ran into her and Riley the day Shelby first joined the soccer team.

"We're here to try to talk you into staying with the team," you tell her.

"But I'm a rotten player," Shelby says.

"We expected too much," Riley says. "How can you play well when you're worried about disappointing us?"

You're grateful to Riley for trying to share the blame, but you know it rests on your shoulders. "I'm sorry I took all the fun out of the game," you say to Shelby. "I was a new player once, too, and I got to be a better player because I had fun on the field. If I had been worried about making mistakes, I never would have stuck with it."

"We need to have more fun," Riley agrees.

"How about if we have a 'fun-only' soccer game?" you ask Shelby. "I promise that if you *don't* have any fun, I won't bug you about staying with the team."

"Can I get that in writing?" Shelby asks.

At first, you think Shelby is serious. Then she smiles. "Okay, I'm in," she says. "Fun only."

 Turn to page 80.

You decide to have your fun-only soccer game in the meadow tomorrow afternoon. You call on your teammates for ideas. Riley suggests a few games she learned at soccer camp. Neely offers to bring her CD player, and Amber says she'll bring a few fun surprises, too.

The next afternoon, the sun is shining, the music is blasting, and you and your teammates are playing "three-legged soccer"—a version of a three-legged race. You and Shelby have partnered up. One of your legs is tied to one of hers with a bandanna, and you're trying to kick the soccer ball with your combined leg, which is nearly *impossible* to do without falling over.

You're untying yourselves and laughing hysterically when Amber runs over with a couple of dogs from Pet-Palooza. Coconut, a little white Westie, and Honey, a golden retriever pup, race after the soccer balls.

"Oh, they're so cute!" you exclaim. Coconut pushes the ball with her nose, while Honey wrestles with it using all four paws.

"Honey can't get a penalty for using her hands," Shelby says with a laugh. "Four legs would make soccer a whole lot easier!"

It's good to hear Shelby laugh again. You're glad she's having fun. *It's all about fun,* you remind yourself. *And it's going to stay that way.*

The End

8

You're not ready to give up yet. "How many of your photographs were this good the first time you picked up a camera?" you ask.

Shelby gives you a half-smile. "None," she admits. "I have gotten better, though, and if I take enough shots, some of them are bound to be good."

"Exactly," you say. "That's how you get to be a good soccer player, too—by playing. No one plays great in their first game. I sure didn't, but I've learned a lot since then. You will, too. Will you stay with the team, Shelby? Please?"

Shelby stares at the photos for a while. Then she turns to you. "Will you still be my coach?" she asks.

This time, you don't hesitate. "I will," you say, "that is, if you'll let me."

You feel a rush of relief when Shelby gives you one of her genuine smiles. "I'd like that," she says.

You hear the rest of the team talking and laughing as they pass the yearbook office on their way to the postgame party. "C'mon," you say to Shelby. "Let's go celebrate before we have to paint the attic."

"Will there be cookies?" Shelby asks with a twinkle in her eye.

You laugh. "Definitely."

"Then let's go!" Shelby says.

After the party—and plenty of cookies—you and Shelby head over to Brightstar House to help paint the attic. As you climb the stairs to the attic, Becca rushes up behind you.

"So what do we have to do to turn the attic into a gym?" she asks.

Shelby looks confused. "A gym?" she asks. "When did we decide that?"

"We haven't—yet," Becca says. "It's what most girls want, though."

Becca just won't let up. She gives you a meaningful look, but you say nothing.

When you reach the attic, someone turns on a radio. You all get to work, painting and singing along to your favorite songs. By working together, you finish painting in just a few hours. The attic looks amazing.

Emmy claps her hands to get everyone's attention. She's about to speak when Becca cuts her off. "So who wants to turn this space into a gym?" she asks.

"I have another idea," Emmy says firmly. "Let's talk to the girls on campus and find out what *they* want. We can meet again in a week to compare ideas."

Everyone—everyone except Becca, that is—agrees.

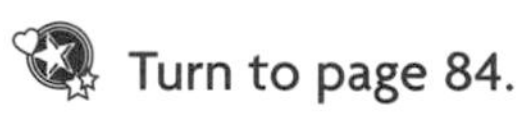
Turn to page 84.

You and Shelby gather girls' opinions whenever you can—around homework and soccer practices. You're both looking forward to the next soccer game, even though it's against one of your toughest competitors.

On Friday night before the game, your coach calls a team meeting to assign positions for Saturday's match. Once again, you and Shelby are playing together. Only this time, you're defenders along with Amber and Paige.

"We'll be the Fantastic Four," says Paige, giving the rest of you high fives.

The next morning, you wake up ready to go. You're so excited about the game that you can barely eat breakfast. You stop by Shelby's room on the way to the sports center. "How are you feeling?" you ask her.

"Excited and *nervous*," Shelby says. "I hope I don't make too many mistakes this time."

"Nobody's perfect. We all make mistakes," you say, quoting Riley's favorite motto. And boy, is she right. You've made your share of mistakes on the field—and in coaching Shelby. You're hoping you do better this time, too.

Riley catches up with you and Shelby just as you're leaving Brightstar House. "Okay, teammates," she says. "We're going to concentrate on having *fun*, right?"

"Right!" you and Shelby say in stereo.

Twenty minutes later, you take the field next to Shelby. The other team wins the coin toss and is about to kick off. "Ready?" you ask Shelby.

"Ready," she says.

Soon you're both running up and down the field, looking for ways to support your teammates or to steal the ball from the other team.

Shelby is in the right place at the right time when the ball shoots out from the middle of a swarm of players. She gets to the ball, but then she hesitates.

 If you encourage her to pass the ball to you, turn to page 90.

 If you encourage her to dribble, turn to page 87.

You can see how sad Shelby is. You can hardly speak around the lump in your throat. "Is that because of me?" you ask.

Shelby pauses for a long moment. "It's not going to be any fun if everyone is just waiting for me to make mistakes," she says.

You know that by *everyone,* Shelby means you. You made a big mess of things. "Are we still friends?" you ask.

"Of course," Shelby says. But there's no sparkle in her hazel eyes, and she doesn't smile. "I have lots of work to do now," Shelby says, "so I guess I'll see you later."

You walk away feeling miserable. You were so focused on winning that you forgot about something much more important—friendship. Now you have a new goal: winning back Shelby's trust. You'll keep trying until you find a way.

The End

"Dribble!" you yell.

Shelby dribbles the ball down the field with you by her side, shouting encouragement and trying to keep the other team from getting too close. Shelby's dribbling is not as fast and tight as it could be, but you, Paige, and Amber all work to block the other team's players. You *are* the Fantastic Four. The other team can't get near Shelby or the ball!

Before you know it, you've protected Shelby so well that she has driven the ball all the way down the field. She's right in front of the goal, a shocked smile on her face.

If you urge Shelby to shoot for the goal, turn to page 88.

If you tell Shelby to pass the ball to Paige, turn to page 91.

"Shoot!" you yell. "Shoot!"

Shelby shoots—and scores! Seconds later the halftime whistle blows. Innerstar U is up 1 to 0.

Shelby's goal gives the entire team confidence for the second half. Your own game seems better than ever as you defend your goal and try to get the ball down the field.

The second half of the game is a shutout—neither team scores. When the final whistle blows, you've won the game. And Shelby made the only goal!

In spite of all your worries about bringing a new player onto the team, Shelby came through and helped to win the game for Innerstar U. All she needed was a chance to shine.

The End

"Pass it to me!" you yell. Shelby does, but you have opponents on either side of you. You need to pass again, or you'll lose the ball. You give the ball a light tap in Shelby's direction. She collects the pass on the run and then passes the ball again, right back to you.

The two of you run up the field, passing the ball back and forth with a series of light taps—just as you did in one of your practice drills. You're both grinning and having fun. It's as if you are the only two players on the field.

When the other team catches on to what you're doing, though, they manage to steal the ball. They drive the ball down the field and take the lead, 1 to 0.

You hope Shelby isn't blaming herself. You couldn't hold on to the ball either. "We'll get 'em next time," you say to her.

Shelby looks worried. You've got to help her relax. You raise both fists in a bodybuilder pose and announce in a wacky accent, "The Fantastic Four will not be defeated."

That draws a smile from her. You bounce on the balls of your feet, ready to start running when the ball is in play again.

Turn to page 92.

You're not sure that Shelby can get the ball into the goal. "Pass!" you yell. "Pass it to Paige."

Shelby does, of course, even though she's in a better position than Paige to make a goal. You're Shelby's coach, and she trusts you.

Paige gives the ball a kick toward the net, but the goalkeeper makes an easy save. As you watch the other team drive the ball down the field, you wonder why you *really* told Shelby to pass the ball. She trusted you, but you didn't trust her. She did a great job dribbling down the field, and she earned her shot at the goal—hit or miss.

You tell yourself that the next time Shelby has an opportunity like that, you'll be a better coach. You'll give your friend a chance to shine.

The End

At halftime, your coach congratulates you and Shelby on your great passing run. Then Riley reminds you and your teammates that you're down by just one goal. This game could still be yours.

When you and Shelby hit the field for the second half, you're both filled with confidence. Every time you catch Shelby's eye, she grins at you. She's having fun, and she's playing better because of it.

In the game's final minute, Shelby passes the ball a little wide to Becca, and the other team steals it. Innerstar U loses the game. Still, when you see Shelby jog off the field with a smile on her face, you feel like a winner.

At the postgame party, Shelby tells everyone what a great coach you are. For the first time, you *feel* like a real coach. You compliment Shelby on her playing, too, and everyone nods—except Becca. She whispers something to one of her friends. Is she criticizing Shelby's playing?

You know that Shelby still has a lot to learn, but you won't put up with anyone saying bad things about her. You head back to Brightstar House with a knot in your stomach.

Rather than going to your own room, you decide to knock on Riley's door. You want to ask her for advice about the Becca situation. When Riley opens her door, you see that she's hanging out with Isabel. That's okay—she may be able to help, too.

"I'm worried about Becca," you say to both girls. "She's been pretty hard on Shelby. Her attitude is making it tough for the rest of us to have fun."

Riley nods. "Becca is too focused on winning," she says. "So are some of the other girls on the team."

"What we need is a mood makeover," Isabel says thoughtfully.

"What about a sleepover?" Riley asks. "We can forget about soccer and just have fun as a team."

Isabel's eyes light up. "A makeover sleepover!" she says. "It'll be like a spa party. We can give our team a makeover inside and out."

The two girls have been talking so fast that you could barely get a word in edgewise. Now they're both looking at you, waiting for you to speak.

"What do you think?" asks Riley. "Will this help make things better with Becca?"

If you're willing to try the sleepover, turn to page 94.

If you think that trying to bond with Becca is a lost cause, turn to page 95.

You're not crazy about the idea of spending time with Becca at a sleepover, but you're willing to give it a try—for Shelby's sake. You tell Riley and Isabel that you're in.

The whole team agrees to come to the sleepover. Shelby seems especially excited. She's still flying high from the last soccer game.

"Do you need help with anything?" Shelby asks Isabel.

"Nope!" Isabel replies. "Riley and I have it covered. Just wear your favorite PJs."

You've been eyeing a new pair for yourself in Pajama Jam, and this is the perfect excuse to buy them. You invite Shelby to go with you to the Shopping Square.

You're about to open the door to Pajama Jam when you spot Becca just inside the store. *Great,* you groan inwardly. You're frozen on the sidewalk, wondering what to do.

 If you go in and say hi to Becca, turn to page 96.

 If you ask Shelby if you can stop at the Girl Gear shop next door, turn to page 100.

You appreciate that Riley and Isabel are trying to help, but you think that hanging out with Becca at a sleepover might make things worse—not better. What if she says something to Shelby about her soccer playing?

"I'm not so sure a sleepover will work," you say to Riley. You tell her that you'll think about it—and you do. It makes for a pretty sleepless night.

The next morning, you head up to the attic for another meeting. Most of the girls are gathered there. Emmy is standing up, writing on a big pad of paper. "Okay," she says. "Let's start sharing the ideas we've heard from other students here at Innerstar U."

Becca doesn't waste a second. "Exercise room!" she shouts. "I've been talking to girls all week, and everyone wants an exercise room right in the dorm."

Emmy nods and writes *exercise room* on the pad.

"With a couple of couches, this room would make a great place for study groups to meet," Logan says.

Becca rolls her eyes.

Neely's response is kinder, but she doesn't love Logan's idea either. "We can study at the library, which is pretty close by," Neely says. "It would be a shame to waste all this great space on studying when we could be dancing!"

When you see Logan's face fall, you decide to speak up. "But everyone studies," you point out. "Not everyone dances—or exercises."

Turn to page 98.

Becca is the last person you want to see. But you *are* teammates, and the point of tonight's sleepover is to bond with her. You put on a smile and walk over to her. "Those are great PJs," you say. "I've had my eye on them, too."

Becca looks surprised. "Really?" she says. "You should get them. We could be pajama twins tonight."

"Or maybe triplets?" Shelby jokes, holding up another pair of the PJs.

Becca laughs and nods enthusiastically. You're surprised that she's being so friendly. Then her smile fades, and she says that she isn't sure that she should even go to the sleepover. "I totally messed up in the last game," Becca confesses. "I thought everyone was mad at me."

Wow. This whole time, you were sure that Becca was blaming Shelby for losing the soccer game. It turns out that she was blaming herself.

"No one's mad at you," you assure Becca. "We've all been too worried about our own mistakes. We really *need* this party, don't we?"

"We do," Shelby agrees. "Pajama triplets?" she asks. She holds out her hand, palm down, inviting you and Becca to join the team cheer.

You put your hand on top of Shelby's, and then you both look up at Becca, expectantly.

Becca's cheeks flush pink with relief. "Pajama triplets," she agrees, adding her warm hand to yours.

The End

"And it's not always convenient to use the library," Logan adds. "Especially at night."

"That's true," Neely says slowly. "But how about an art studio?"

Neely's idea gives you one. "Could we—"

Becca cuts you off. "That's silly," she says. "You already have Sparkle Studios. Why do you need another art studio?"

Neely speaks before you can. She throws her arm over her forehead and says dramatically, "Because sometimes inspiration strikes in the middle of the night, and I simply *must* dance or paint or sing!"

Everyone laughs, but you think Neely's on the right track. The Innerstar U campus has everything you need, but sometimes you just want to hang out at Brightstar House instead of going to the library, the art studios, or the sports center.

Becca shoots down Paige's idea—to turn the attic into a mini greenhouse—as soon as she raises her hand.

Emmy writes *greenhouse* on the pad anyway, after *exercise room, study zone,* and *art and dance studio.*

Riley likes Becca's idea. She would love to be able to work out without having to go all the way across campus to the sports center.

Shelby looks around the attic. "This would make a great place for sleepovers and for watching DVDs," she says.

Isabel thinks it would be fun to create a play space for pets that visit from Pet-Palooza.

When you're finished brainstorming, Emmy has six main ideas on the list.

"Those are all good ideas. How are we going to choose just one?" Logan asks. "Do we vote? Draw straws?"

If you want to take a vote, turn to page 101.

If you want to hear everyone talk about their choices first, turn to page 104.

Shelby's confused by your sudden change of plans, but she follows you into Girl Gear. You pretend to be wildly interested in yoga pants while you keep one eye on the window.

When you see Becca leaving Pajama Jam, you breathe a sigh of relief. You weren't ready to have a conversation with her. At least at the sleepover tonight, the rest of your teammates will be there, too.

You and Shelby buy matching PJs at Pajama Jam, and you spend the rest of the afternoon helping Isabel and Riley get ready for the sleepover. Isabel transforms her room into a mini spa, complete with a hair-styling station and a place for facials. She puts on some soothing tunes, and she spreads colorful, comfy pillows and fashion magazines on the floor around the room.

Turn to page 102.

"Let's vote," you say. "Everybody who wants to turn the attic into a study zone, raise your hand."

Logan raises her hand. So do you.

"That's two for a study zone," says Emmy, marking the votes on the board. "Who wants an exercise room?" she asks.

Two hands go up—Riley's and Becca's. Becca waves her hand high in the air, as if that will make Emmy count it twice.

You realize now that voting so quickly wasn't the best plan. It already looks as if you'll end up with a tie vote.

"Maybe we'd better talk about the ideas for a while, and then vote," you suggest.

Turn to page 104.

When the other girls arrive, Riley says that there's just one rule for the sleepover: "You can't talk about winning or losing," she says. "If you use the word *win* or *lose*, you have to put a quarter in the fun jar."

Shelby laughs. "We should make that rule in soccer, too," she says. "When I focus on having fun, I play *better*."

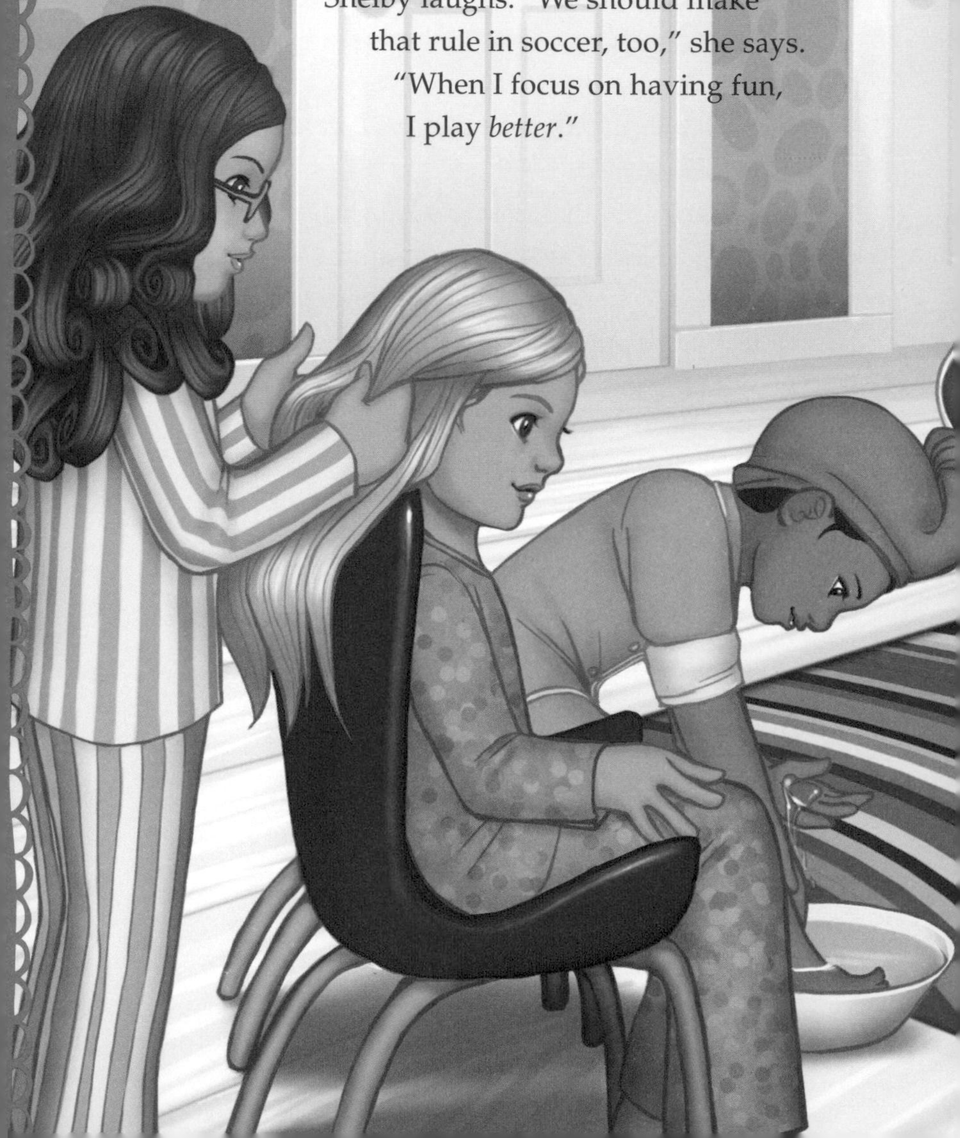

For the next few hours, you and your teammates do just that. You have fun doing each other's hair. You spread masks on your faces and smile for Shelby's camera. You tear out pictures of clothes from magazines to make "dream outfits." When you see Becca's dream outfit, you discover you have the same taste in clothing. Who knew?

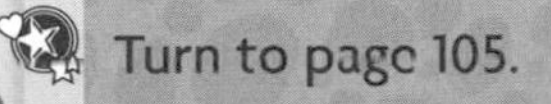
Turn to page 105.

"Who wants to talk about a place for pets?" Emmy asks.

Isabel is about to speak up for her idea when Amber raises her hand. "It's fun when we get to pet-sit animals right here at Brightstar House," she says. "But they come for pretty short visits. We wouldn't need this whole space."

Emmy turns to Shelby. "Do you want to talk more about your idea?" she asks.

Shelby looks around the attic. "It would be great to come up here for sleepovers and parties," she says, "but that doesn't mean we can't use the room for other things."

Paige agrees. "Some plants would brighten up this space," she says, "but I don't need the *whole* attic for my plants. I already have a jungle in my room."

Everyone giggles at that. You can tell that you and your friends are starting to think alike. "Why don't we all share the space?" you ask. "Like we share the soccer field with other sports."

 Turn to page 106.

By the time you're all cozy in your sleeping bags and ready to go to sleep, you're feeling like true teammates. You only hope that you can carry this team spirit to next week's game—the final game of the season. You sure would like to end the season with a great game, win or lose.

Team spirit is definitely riding high during the attic meeting the next morning. Everyone is sharing ideas, and even Becca is listening to what others have to say. Emmy writes down all the ideas on a big pad of paper.

Turn to page 99.

"Great idea," Neely says. "We could have a cupboard for art supplies. And if there's not too much furniture, we could come up here and dance whenever we want to." She grins at Logan. "I mean, whenever girls aren't up here studying or gazing at the stars."

Logan grins back at her. Then she looks at Becca and Riley—they wanted to turn the space into an exercise room.

"We could put a couple of yoga mats in that cupboard," Riley offers. "We don't need the whole attic."

Becca is silent for a minute, but then even she agrees. "I guess it would be pretty hard to get a treadmill up those stairs," she admits. "Besides, if I don't want to go to the sports center for a workout, I can always come up here and dance with Neely."

Neely laughs, twirls over to Becca, and draws her into a dance. "Any time," she says.

"So did we make a decision?" you ask. "Should we turn the attic into a place where we can all come to hang out, study, dance, or whatever?"

"Let's do it," Emmy says. Everyone else nods, too.

"Woo-hoo!" Neely says. "We could even have our end-of-season soccer party here."

"Great idea!" says Riley. "That'll be here before we know it."

She's right. You're excited about the final game, but you're a little sad that soccer's coming to an end, too.

Turn to page 118.

You don't agree with Riley, but you say nothing. As the rain comes down, the grass gets muddy. Soon everyone on the field is covered in brown polka dots.

When you see the bully on the other team trip Shelby again, you've had it. You lock eyes with Becca. You're pretty sure she's thinking the same thing you are. Then you set off after the bully. You're running fast, and the grass is slick. Before you know it, you're sliding face-first in the mud. You look up just in time to see Emmy block the bully's shot at a goal.

After that, you can't seem to stay out of the mud. Your uniform turns brown—along with your hair, your face, and every other part of you. The ref finally throws the bully out of the game and Innerstar U wins, but you can't take credit for that. You spent most of the game in the muddy muck.

After the final whistle, you plop down on the bench next to Becca. Her own face is streaked with mud, and she still looks a little mad.

Neither one of you says a word. But as Becca eyes your uniform, she finally cracks a smile.

"Talk about dirty play," she says with a giggle.

That cracks you up, too. It feels good to laugh with Becca, but you've both learned your lesson. Next time, you'll focus on playing fair—and clean!

The End

You're furious, and your teammates are, too—especially Becca. You overhear her tell Riley that she's going to get even.

"The best way to get even is to score goals," Riley says. "I don't want to win if we can't play fair."

"But it's not fair to let the other team cheat their way to a win," you pipe up. "Shelby's worked too hard. We all have."

"If we play dirty too, that makes us just as bad as they are," Riley says. "Let's show them that we can win by out-playing them, not by out-cheating them."

If you still agree with Becca, turn to page 110.

If you listen to Riley instead, turn to page 112.

You can't stand watching Shelby get pushed around, but what can you do? You're playing goalkeeper, which means you can't help Shelby out on the field.

You watch Shelby chase after a pass, and you can see the bully getting ready to zero in on her again. Then, from out of nowhere, Becca sprints forward and blocks the bully with her elbow so that Shelby can intercept the ball.

The ref doesn't see Becca, but your coach does. Right away, she pulls Becca out of the game. Becca takes a seat on the sidelines. She's fuming. A part of you is grateful to her for standing up for Shelby, but now that Becca is out of the game, you'll have to figure out how to protect Shelby yourself.

Turn to page 114.

The rain cools your temper and calms you down. Riley said a clean win was the best way to get back at the other team, and she's right. You see how focused your team is on winning, and no one is more determined than Shelby right now. She scores the goal that puts Innerstar U in the lead.

"Yes!" Shelby yells, pumping her fist in the air. She gives a big smile to the girl who tripped her, as if to say, "Look what happens when you play *fair*."

When the final whistle blows, Innerstar U is still ahead by one goal—Shelby's! Your win probably stings the other team even more because Innerstar U played a clean game. They couldn't beat you even when they cheated.

You've been teaching Shelby how to play soccer, but she and Riley just taught you an important lesson about being a good sport. They insisted on playing fair. You could have matched the other team's fouls with fouls of your own, but that wouldn't have led to a win—at least not to the kind of win that you can be proud of.

The End

Riley's right. Playing dirty will only bring you down to the other team's level. You don't want a win unless it's a clean win.

Shelby's anger seems to be good for her soccer skills. The rest of your team is fired up too, and soon Innerstar U is leading 3 to 1. The bully gets more reckless in a desperate attempt to win, and this time she gets caught.

Shelby gets a penalty kick, and she sends it right into the goal. When the final whistle blows, the entire team rushes to Shelby, lifts her off the ground, and carries her off the field. It always feels good to win, but this win is even sweeter because you all played clean.

Just as you're packing up to leave, the sun peeks out from behind the clouds—as if it wants to celebrate with you. Riley calls everyone together for a quick meeting.

"Who wants to plan the end-of-season party?" she asks.

You and Shelby both raise your hands. So does Becca. You cringe. Becca has come a long way as a teammate, but you remember how hard it was to work with her on the attic committee.

If you leave your hand up in the air, go online to innerstarU.com/secret and enter this code: TRY2BFAIR

If you bow out and let Becca plan the party without you, turn to page 116.

Your coach asks you to take over Becca's position while Emmy takes over as goalkeeper. As you walk past Riley, she says, "Now, remember—we're going to win by playing a clean game."

You shake your head. "I'm not sure we can win that way," you tell her. "That other team is sneaky. They make sure the ref can't see them when they pull their dirty tricks, and they're being really mean to Shelby."

"They'll slip up and get caught," Riley promises you. "If you pull any dirty tricks of your own, the ref will pull you out of the game—or Coach will have to."

A gentle rain starts to fall as you consider Riley's words.

If you decide to take Riley's advice and play clean, turn to page 111.

If you still want to try to get even with the other team, turn to page 108.

The first message you see written on your poster is from Becca. "To the best sport on the team," the note reads. "I'm glad we're teammates and friends. XOXO, Becca."

You suddenly wish that Becca's note were true—that you had been a better friend to her. The truth is, you've been tough on Becca. She was a little hard to take when Shelby first joined the team, but since then, she's worked hard to be a kinder friend and teammate. She deserves a second chance.

You pick up a marker and walk over to the poster-sized photo of Becca. She's running down the field, her hair blowing in the wind behind her. She looks happy—the same way you feel when you're playing.

"Can't wait to play with you again next season," you write. And you mean it.

The End

You don't help plan the party, but you *do* look forward to the celebration. A couple of days beforehand, you head up to check out the redecorated attic. You're proud of the space. Working together, you and your friends turned it into a super-cool hangout. Innerstar U gave you a couple of comfy sofas, a TV, a DVD player, and a table you can use for crafts or studying. Plus, there are cabinets for storing art supplies and yoga mats.

Paige filled the windows with green plants, and Isabel brought up some colorful pillows. Neely painted a small mural in Innerstar U colors, and Shelby hung some of her fabulous photographs. Becca brought up exercise DVDs so that girls can work out. There's something from every one of your friends in this room—and something *for* every girl, too. That's what makes it so perfect.

It's even more perfect the night of the party. A banner hangs at the top of the stairs that says, "Welcome to the All-Star Party." Shelby and Becca hung twinkling white lights along the walls. Shelby made poster-sized photos of each girl, or "star," on the team. When you step into the room, you see your teammates writing notes to one another on the posters.

If you go check out your own poster, turn to page 115.

If you stop to say hi to Shelby first, turn to page 119.

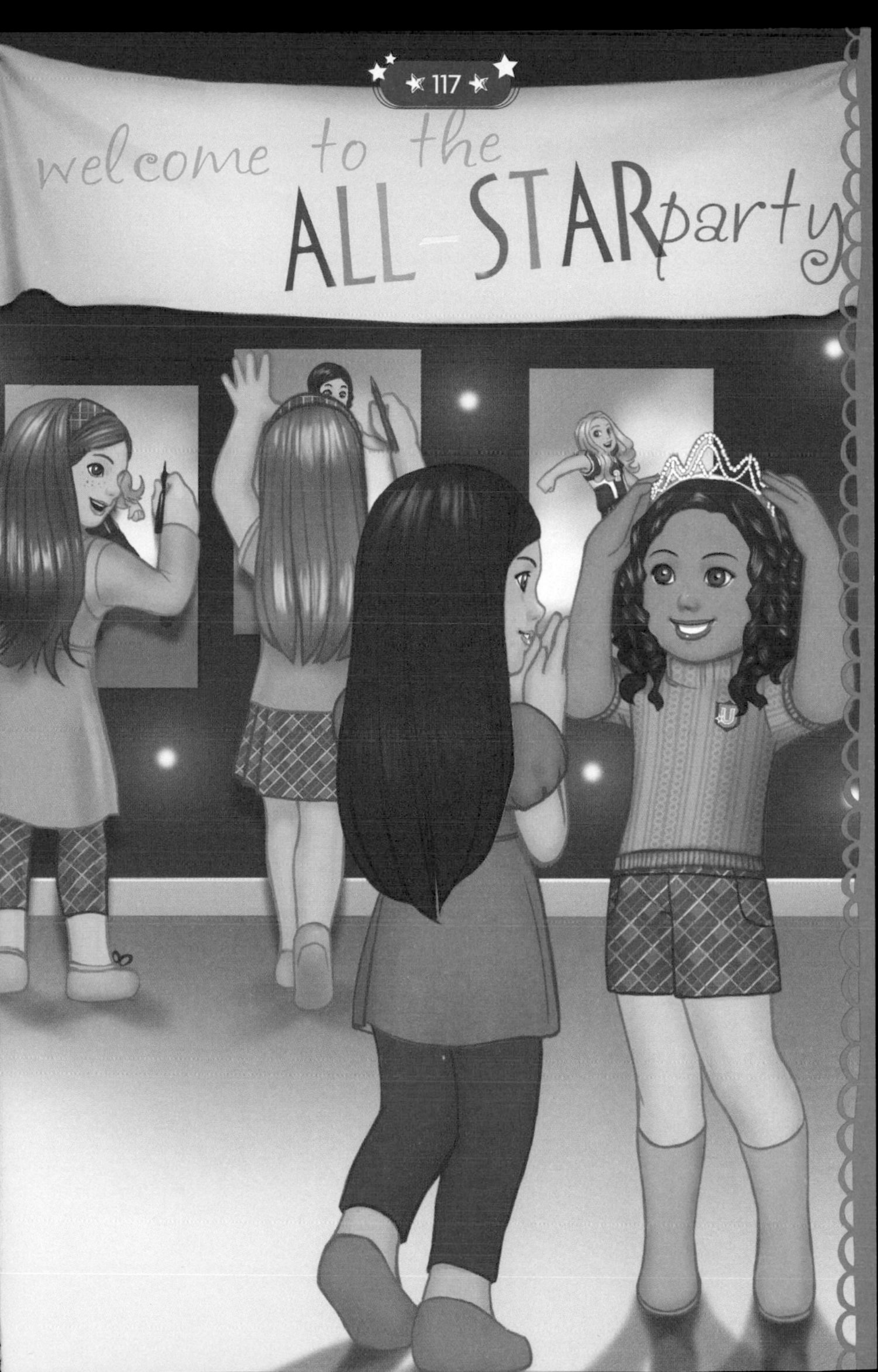
welcome to the
ALL-STAR party

The morning of the final soccer game, you're flying high. You're excited about playing with your friends and celebrating with them at the end-of-season party. When your coach asks you to be goalkeeper, you happily pull on the keeper's gloves and jersey.

Shelby is playing forward. It's the first time you haven't played right next to each other. It feels a little weird to be separated, but at least you can hang back now and watch Shelby play.

You're watching from your position near the net when you see Shelby steal the ball and pass it to Paige. Shelby is lightning quick. You can't believe it! She sprints past the other team's defenders to collect the ball from Paige on the other side.

Shelby is about to take a shot at the goal when a defender from the other team trips her—on purpose. She's sprawled out on the field while the other girl steals the ball and dribbles it down the field.

 Turn to page 109.